𝕾uperphonics *Storybooks* will help you learn to read using Ruth Miskin's highly effective phonic method. Each story is fun to read and has been carefully written to include particular sounds and spellings.

The Storybooks are graded so your child can progress with confidence from easy words to harder ones. There are four levels - Blue (the easiest), Green, Purple and Turquoise (the hardest). Each level is linked to one of the core *Superphonics Books*.

ISBN 0 340 77354 5

Text copyright © Gill Munton 2001
Illustrations copyright © Michael Reid 2001

Editorial by Gill Munton
Design by Sarah Borny

The rights of Gill Munton and Michael Reid to be identified as the author and illustrator of this Work have been asserted by them in accordance with the Copyright, Designs and Patents Act 1988.

First published in Great Britain 2001

10 9 8 7 6 5 4 3 2

First published in 2001 by Hodder Children's Books, a division of Hodder Headline Limited, 338 Euston Road, London NW1 3BH

Printed in Hong Kong by Wing King Tong

A CIP record is registered by and held at the British Library.

Target words

All the Blue Storybooks focus on the following sounds:

a as in **cat**   **e** as in **wet**
i as in **bin**   **o** as in **fox**
u as in **bug**

These target words are featured in the book:

at	Tag	big	box	bug
bath	van	bin	fog	bus
cat(s)	bed	dish	fox	fun
fat	den	fish	hot	hut
hat	get	his	log	Mum
lap	hen	in	lot(s)	pup
Mag	Jem	Jim	Mog	rug
man	Ned	Sim	nod	shut
map	net	sit	on	sun
mat	Red	Tig	pop	us
nap	shed	tin	pot	yum
path	wet	with	shop	
Sam				

Other words

Also included are some common words (e.g. **and**, **go**) which your child will be learning in his or her first few years at school.

A few other words have been used to help the story to flow.

Reading the book

1 Make sure you and your child are sitting in a quiet, comfortable place.

2 Tell him or her a little about the stories, without giving too much away:

This is a book about lots of cats, who get into lots of mischief!

This will give your child a mental picture; having a context for a story makes it easier to read the words.

3 Read the target words (above) together. This will mean that you can both enjoy the stories without having to spend too much time working out the words. Help your child to sound out each word (e.g. **c-a-t**) before saying the whole word.

4 Let your child read each of the stories aloud. Help him or her with any difficult words and discuss the story as you go along. Stop now and again to ask your child to predict what will happen next. This will help you to see whether he or she has understood what has happened so far.

Above all, enjoy the stories, and praise your child's reading!

Ruth Miskin's
Superphonics

Blue Storybook

Lots of Cats

by Gill Munton

Illustrated by Michael Reid

a division of Hodder Headline Limited

P
MVN

Tig

Tag

Nod

Ned

Sim

Sam

Mag

Mog

Jim

Jem

Tig and Tag
on the path

Tig and Tag
in the bath

6

Tig and Tag
with Big Red Mum

Tig and Tag say
Yum, yum, yum!

Tig and Tag
see a hut

They can't
get in!
The hut
is shut!

Tig and Tag
on the bus

Tig and Tag say

Look at us!

Nod and Ned
on the shed

Nod and Ned
in my bed

Nod and Ned
on the mat

Nod and Ned
in my hat

Nod and Ned
with a
big fat hen

Nod and Ned
see a fox
in his den

Nod and Ned
sit on a log

Nod and Ned
sit in the fog

Sim and Sam
get a net

Sim and Sam
get wet,
wet, wet!

14

Sim and Sam
see a fish

Sim and Sam
at the dish

Sim and Sam
in the sun

Sim and Sam
have fun,
fun, fun!

Sim and Sam
see a pup

Sim and Sam go

up, up, up!

Mag and Mog
sit on a rug

Mag and Mog
see a bug

Mag and Mog
in the pot

Mag and Mog get
hot, hot, hot!

Mag and Mog
see a tin

Mag and Mog
go in the bin

20

Mag and Mog
see the fox

Mag and Mog
in a box

Jim and Jem
see a man

Jim and Jem
get in his van

Jim and Jem
in a shop

Jim and Jem go

Pop! Pop! Pop!

Lots of cats
need a nap

Lots of cats
on my lap